Old Friends, New Friends

For my Dad—who treasures his friends,
old and new—P. H.

LITTLE SIMON
An imprint of Simon & Schuster Children's Publishing Division
1230 Avenue of the Americas
New York, New York 10020
Copyright © 2002 by Simon & Schuster, Inc.
The names and depictions of Raggedy Ann and Raggedy Andy are trademarks of Simon & Schuster.
All rights reserved, including the right of reproduction in whole or in part in any form.
READY-TO-READ, LITTLE SIMON, and colophon are registered trademarks of Simon & Schuster.
Manufactured in the United States of America
First Edition
2 4 6 8 10 9 7 5 3 1

The Library of Congress has cataloged the library edition as follows:

Library of Congress Cataloging-in-Publication Data
Hall, Patricia.
Raggedy Ann & Andy : old friends, new friends / by Patricia Hall ;
illustrated by Alison Winfield.— 1st ed.
p. cm.—(Raggedy Ann & Andy) (Ready-to-read)
Summary: Marcella teaches Raggedy Ann and Raggedy Andy the fun of making
new friends and the importance of keeping old ones.
ISBN 0-689-85225-8 (lib ed)
ISBN 0-689-85224-X (pbk)
[1. Friendship—Fiction. 2. Dolls—Fiction.] I. Title: Raggedy Ann and Andy. II.
Winfield, Alison, ill. III. Title. IV. Series. V. Classic Raggedy Ann & Andy
PZ7.H147515 Raj 2002
[E]—dc21
2002000943

CLASSIC
Raggedy Ann & Andy

Old Friends, New Friends

by Patricia Hall
illustrated by Alison Winfield

Ready-to-Read

Little Simon

New York   London   Toronto   Sydney   Singapore

Marcella held Raggedy Ann

and Raggedy Andy

in her arms.

"I am meeting my friends

at the park!"

she said.

"Kate is my friend

from last year.

Lucy is a new girl in school,"

said Marcella

to her doll friends.

The dolls liked friends.

While Marcella waited

for her friends

she sang a song.

"Make new friends,

but keep the old.

One is silver

and the other is gold."

Marcella ran to meet

Kate and Lucy.

"Can friends **really**

be silver?"

asked Raggedy Andy.

"Or gold?" asked the Camel

with the Wrinkled Knees.

"That must be people talk

for something **very** special,"

said Raggedy Ann.

Lucy and Kate

each held a doll.

"Oh, boy!"

whispered Raggedy Andy.

"We can make

new friends too!"

 13

"Let's swing first,"

said Lucy.

"Then we can play catch,"

said Marcella.

"We can build

sand houses, too!"

laughed Kate.

The girls played together

all morning.

Then Mama called,

"Lunchtime!"

Raggedy Andy stood up.

"Hi, I am Raggedy Andy,"

he said.

He felt a little shy.

"My name is Bobby!"

said Kate's doll.

"And I am Alice!"

said Lucy's doll.

 19

"I am Raggedy Ann.

I like your glasses."

"Thank you!"

said Alice.

"They are **silver**!"

"My name is Uncle Clem.

Your buttons are shiny."

"Do you like them?"

asked Bobby.

"They are **gold**!"

Soon nobody felt

shy anymore.

The dolls told stories

and they ran

and jumped around.

Alice picked some flowers

and gave them

to Uncle Clem.

Later the girls

played with their dolls.

Then it was time

to go home.

"Good-bye, Kate!

See you later, Lucy!"

That night

Marcella kissed her dolls.

"I had fun with

Kate and Lucy today,"

she said.

Marcella sang her song

again.

"Make new friends,

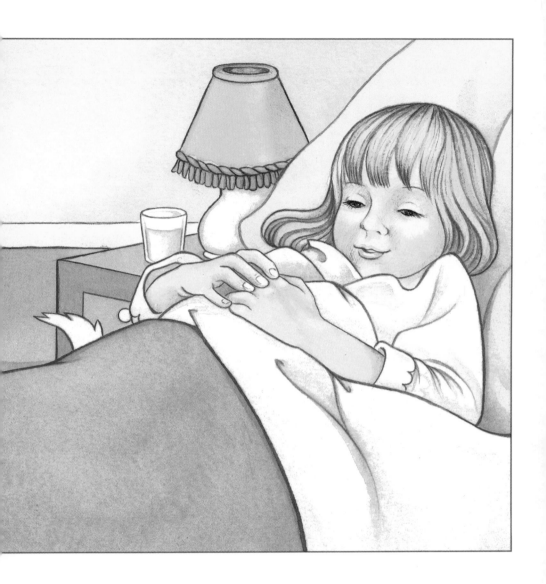

but keep the old.

One is silver

and the other is gold."

Later

Raggedy Ann

sat up in bed.

"**I** know what

Marcella's song means!"

she whispered.

"Silver and gold are different.

But they each are special."

"New friends and old friends

are different.

But they are each

special, too!

Just like all of **us**!"

giggled Raggedy Andy.

And with that,

all the dolls

fell fast asleep

to dream about

their old and new friends.